WHAT CAN YOU DO WITH A SHOE?

by the author and artist of
THE GIANT STORY

WHAT CAN YOU DO

WITH A SHOE?

by Beatrice Schenk de Regniers

Pictures by Maurice Sendak

HARPER & ROW, PUBLISHERS NEW YORK, EVANSTON, AND LONDON

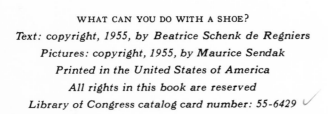

WHAT CAN YOU DO WITH A SHOE?
Text: copyright, 1955, by Beatrice Schenk de Regniers
Pictures: copyright, 1955, by Maurice Sendak
Printed in the United States of America
Library of Congress catalog card number: 55-6429

for fun

What can you do

What can you do

What can you do

with a shoe?

You can put it on your ear

On your beery-leery ear,

You can put it on your ear, tra-la

Or wear it on your head

Or butter it like bread

Or use apple jam instead, ha ha

Oh, stop all that nonsense!

What do you *really* do with your shoes?

Of course!

What can you do

What can you do

What can you do

with a chair?

You can pretend you are a bear   saying boo   in a zoo

Or a seasick kangaroo   (Now the chair is a cano

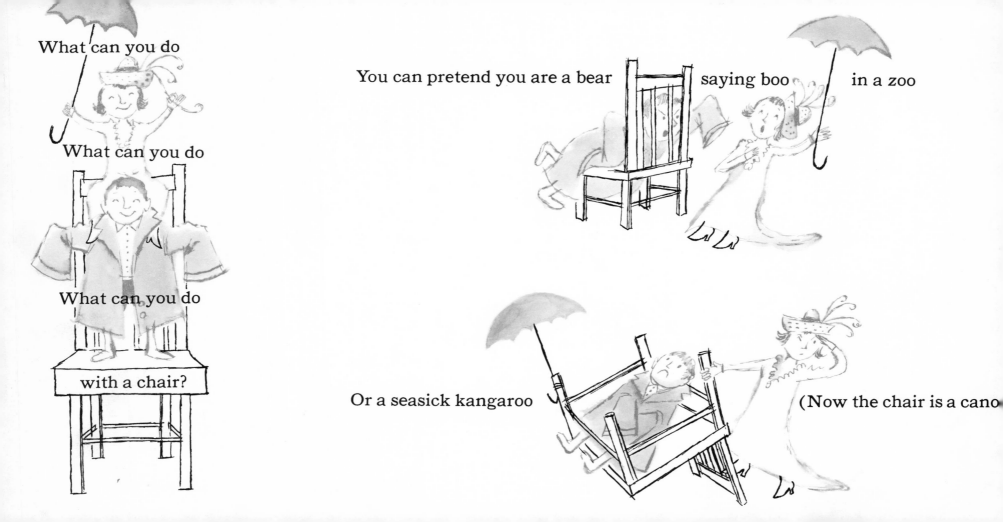

Or use it for a table
When you're sitting on the floor

Or if you are able
Shove it up against the door

So *nobody* can get in unless you say so.

Or it's an aeroplane

Or a train   And you're going on a journey to the MOON.

Now Really!

Is that what you're *supposed to do*
    with a chair?

What do *most* people do with chairs?

That's right!

What can you do   What can you do   What can you do   with a hat?

You can fill it up
with pickles

Or with popcorn

Or with glue.

An octopus could rest in it

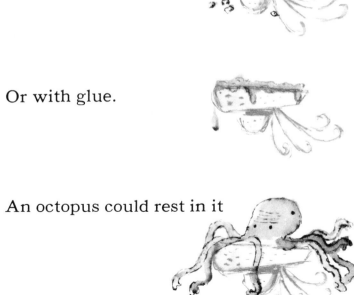

A bird could build a nest in it

A turtle be a guest in it . . . .

Or would a horse look best in it?

Oh, don't be so silly!
What *do* you do with your hat?

Just what everybody does!

What can you do   What can you do   What can you do   with a cup?

You can gobble it up!

Gobble gobble gobble   gubble gubble gubble

Crunch!

Yummy! What a lunch!

Who ever heard of eating cups for lunch?

Or even for breakfast?

You know what people do with cups

don't you?

Drink milk

Or tea

Or coffee

r orange juice.

Things like that.

Now that makes *sense!*

What can you do

What can you do

What can you do

with a broom?

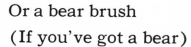

You can use it for a hair brush

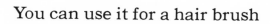

Or a tooth brush

Or a bear brush
(If you've got a bear)

You can use it for a shoe brush

Or a glue brush

Or a chair brush
(I'm sure you've got a chair)

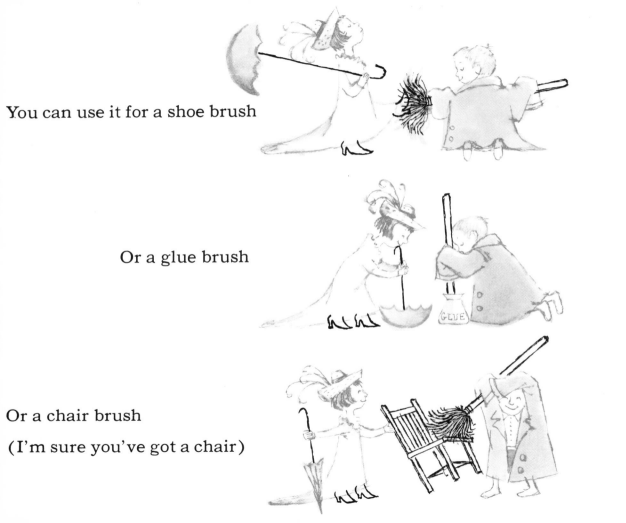

Now a broom would feel real tickly

to a prickly porcupion

And it would seem quite scratchy

on the batchy of a lion.

What on EARTH are you talking about?

Just tell me what you do with a broom.

What does your mother do with a broom?

Hmm. That's what I thought.

What can you do

What can you do

What can you do

with a bed?

Paint it red!

Paint it red   yellow   blue

And paint the covers too!

Paint purple   orange   brown on it

And then jump up and down on it!

Oh, no! No! NO!

What are beds for really?

That's right!   Good night . . . sleep tight!